SANTA'S SURPRISE BOOK

by
JOAN POTTER ELWART

illustrated by
FLORENCE SARAH WINSHIP

GOLDEN PRESS
Western Publishing Company, Inc.
Racine, Wisconsin

Eighth Printing, 1978

One night before Christmas
old Santa sat rocking,

Wondering what he could
stuff in each stocking.

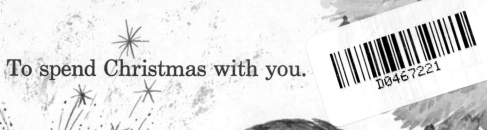

To spend Christmas with you.

One night before Christmas
old Santa sat rocking.

Then he hopped
in this book—

before Christmas
old Santa sat rocking,

"Wait," shouted Santa.
"There's a last thing to do. . . ."

"It's surely a strange one,"
the puzzled elves said.

Here's my wonderful, magical,
stocking-sized book."

He had always left candy
and nuts, it is true.

But this year he wanted
to leave something new.

What could he make that was merry and gay . . .
something surprising for Christmas day?
He had an idea! Santa laughed with delight.

He ran to his shop
and worked there all night.

He found paper and scissors
and thread and some glue,
Some paints—lots of red—
a little of blue.

He took ink and some cardboard

and scissored and snipped.

He glued and he stitched

and he dabbled and dripped.

Santa called in his elves
the next night and said, "Look!